♡ Eva's New Pet ♡

Read more OWL DIARIES books!

OWL DIARIES

♡ Eva's New Pet ♡

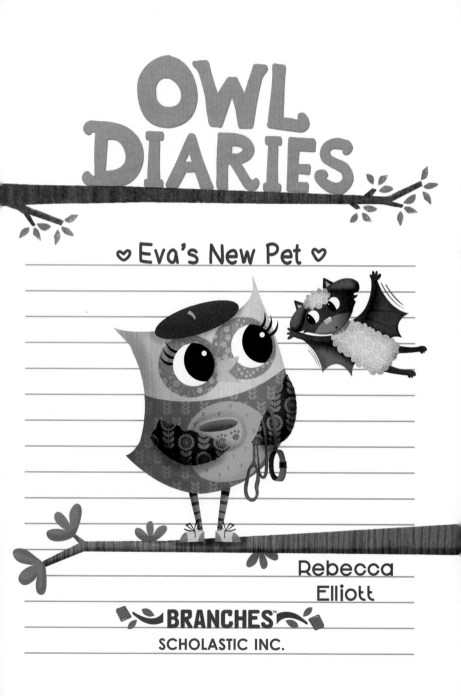

Rebecca
Elliott

BRANCHES

SCHOLASTIC INC.

For Miracle, the little dog born
on a very special day. —R.E.

Library of Congress Cataloging-in-Publication Data

Names: Elliott, Rebecca, author, illustrator. | Elliott, Rebecca. Owl diaries ; 15.
Title: Eva's new pet / Rebecca Elliott.
Description: First edition. | New York : Branches/Scholastic Inc., 2021. |
Series: Owl diaries ; 15 | Summary: Eva is excited because
her parents have agreed to let her get a new pet,
but she is not sure what kind of pet to get—or how Baxter, her
bat, will react to a new member of the family.
Identifiers: LCCN 2020048666 (print) | LCCN 2020048667 (ebook) |
ISBN 9781338745375 (paperback) | ISBN 9781338745382 (library binding) |
ISBN 9781338745399 (ebook)
Subjects: LCSH: Owls—Juvenile fiction. | Pets—Juvenile fiction. |
Decision making—Juvenile fiction. | Diaries—Juvenile fiction. | CYAC:
Owls—Fiction. | Pets—Fiction. | Decision making—Fiction. | Diaries—Fiction.
Classification: LCC PZ7.E45812 Euo 2021 (print) | LCC PZ7.E45812 (ebook)
| DDC 823.92 [Fic]—dc23
LC record available at https://lccn.loc.gov/2020048666
LC ebook record available at https://lccn.loc.gov/2020048667

10 9 8 7 6 5 4 3 2 1   21 22 23 24 25

Printed in China   62
First edition, October 2021

Edited by Rachel Matson
Book design by Marissa Asuncion

♡ Table of Contents ♡

♡ A Friend for Baxter ♡

 Sunday

Hi Diary,

   It's me, the one and only Eva the owl! I am SUPER excited this week. I have been asking Mom and Dad for a new pet for ages. And they finally said yes! There are a few things I'll need to do around the tree house before that happens. But first, let me tell you some fun things about myself!

<u>I love:</u>

Picnics

Bing-a-ling-a-ling!

Ringing Barry
the Bell

The word <u>unicorn</u>

Chocolate
milkshakes

When Baxter performs his best trick

How cute Baxter is when he's asleep

BAXTER

z z z

How Baxter gives me cuddles when I am upset

Baxter's kindness to other creatures

I DO NOT love:

When Humphrey's pet
spider Malcolm comes
on our picnics

Bing-a-Ling-a-Ling!

When I haven't
rung Barry the
Bell in a long time

The word
underpants

Bug juice

4

When I don't have
time to play with
Baxter

When Baxter
won't sleep

Baxter feeling
sad when I fly
to school

Baxter feeling
lonely when he's
home alone

This is a picture of when I first got Baxter. Isn't he cute? We adopted him from a bat rescue center.

♥ Baxter's Welcome Home ♥

And here is Baxter now!

I don't think he understands. But I can't wait to see his face when I finally get my new pet!

Being an owl is **FLAP-TASTIC**. So is being a bat! Just like bats, we're nocturnal. That means we sleep during the day and wake up at night.

We can both fly like feathery superheroes.

Owls can see really well. Bats can't, but they use noises to know where everything is.

Owls are <u>birds</u> and feathery. Bats are <u>mammals</u> and furry. We're both cuddly!

I live in a blue and red tree house on Woodpine Avenue in Treetopolis.

My best friend Lucy lives in the orange tree house next door.

11

9

We both go to Treetop Owlementary.
Here's a picture of my class:

Zac
Lilly   Me
Sue   Kiera
Lucy

Zara   Jacob   George
      Carlos   Hailey   Macy
                                    Mrs.
                              Featherbottom

Tomorrow I need to finish doing my list
of chores. Then I can choose a new friend
for Baxter. I can't wait, Diary!

♡ Chores for a Cause ♡

Monday

Before school I cleaned the whole kitchen. Now the tree house is sparkly clean and tidy for my new pet.

Here is my chore list. I only have two jobs left to do!

~~Scrub the toilet (yuck!)~~

~~Do the laundry~~

~~Fly out the trash~~

~~Vacuum the feathers from our carpets~~

~~Tidy my bedroom~~

~~Clean the kitchen~~

Wash the windows

Sweep the dead leaves from our branch

On the way to school I told Lucy I was almost done with my chores.

That's <u>wing-credible</u>, Eva! Do you want me to help after school?

Thank you, Lucy! That would be great!

At school I told the whole class that I would be getting a new pet. Everyone was super excited, including Mrs. Featherbottom!

That gives me an idea. Let's make this week Pet Week! Tomorrow you can all bring in your pets for show-and-tell. On Thursday we'll have a pet fashion parade. And on Friday we'll have a picnic with our pets!

Yay!

PET WEEK
Tuesday - Show-and-Tell
Thursday - Fashion Parade
Friday - Picnic

How exciting, Diary. A whole Pet Week at school! Baxter's going to love playing with the other pets. AND as a thank-you for giving Mrs. Featherbottom the idea, she let me ring Barry the Bell for recess!

After school, Lucy and I went back to my tree house to finish the last two chores. Her pet lizard Rex came too.

When we finished, we had a water fight!

It's amazing how much fun chores can be when you do them with friends!

We told Mom and Dad we'd finished the chores.

That's great, Eva!

We're so proud!

So, I'm dying to know, Eva. What pet are you going to choose?

That's when I realized something. I'd been so excited about getting a new pet, I hadn't decided which one to get!

Oh. I don't know.

We bought you a book to help you choose.

Wow, thank you!

Which PET is best for YOU?

Lucy and I looked through the book together.

So, what do you think, Eva? Which pet IS best for you?

I don't know. They're all so cute! And it's not just about me. I want to get the right friend for Baxter, too.

We wrote a list:

My new pet must be: ?

☐ Cute

☐ Cuddly ?

☐ Friendly ?

☐ Good at playing with Baxter

☐ Not too big (Baxter gets scared easily!)

☐ Not too small (I'd totally lose it!)

The list helps, but I still don't know which pet will tick all the boxes. I hope I get some ideas from pet show-and-tell tomorrow!

♡ Which Pet to Get ♡

School was so much fun tonight! We all brought in our pets. Mrs. Featherbottom had us stand up and share one reason why we think our pet is the best.

PET WEEK

Tuesday - Show-and-Tell
Thursday - Fashion Par...
Friday - Picnic

Chester is the softest pet ever because he's so fluffy!

Lady is the most fabulous pet because she lets me decorate her shell.

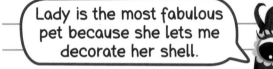

Then it was my turn to talk about Baxter. There were so many reasons why he was the best pet. I couldn't decide on just one!

Suddenly, Zara's crab started walking sideways . . . and almost fell off the table! But Baxter caught her just in time.

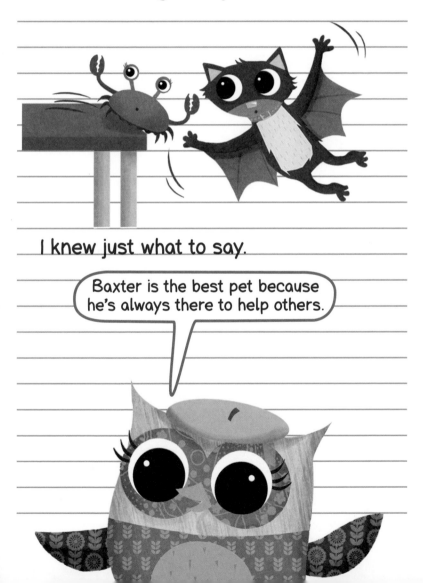

I knew just what to say.

Baxter is the best pet because he's always there to help others.

At recess Lucy asked me if show-and-tell helped me decide which type of pet to adopt. I thought about the list we made.

My new pet must be:

□ Cute

□ Cuddly

□ Friendly

□ Good at playing with Baxter

□ Not too big (Baxter gets scared easily!)

□ Not too small (I'd totally lose it!)

I don't know, they're all so friendly. I think the most important thing is which pet Baxter will get along with best.

We all sat down in a circle with our pets. Baxter sat in the middle. We waited to see who he would want to play with.

But then Baxter really surprised us — he didn't start to play with any of the pets! He just looked grumpy.

And then he flew off and hid inside a tree!

Lucy and I followed Baxter.

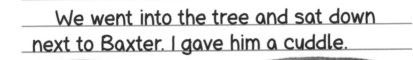

We went into the tree and sat down next to Baxter. I gave him a cuddle.

I'm sorry if I put you on the spot, Baxter.

Maybe Baxter would be more comfortable playing with the pets at home.

I told the class my pet-sitting idea. They all thought it sounded great!

Do you want me to help out, too? I think a whole class of pets might be quite a <u>wing-ful</u>.

That would be great! Thank you, Hailey!

Yes! But all the pets are so good, I don't think it will be <u>that</u> difficult.

After lunch we worked on a really fun project.

Time to start making your pets their costumes for the fashion parade on Thursday! I want them to look like farm animals!

I brought Baxter's costume home so I could keep working on it. I've decided to dress him up as a sheep. He'll look so cuddly with all that wool!

Oh, and great news. I asked Mom and Dad, and they said it's okay to pet-sit tomorrow! I will just need to clean up afterward.

I can't wait, Diary!

♡ Too Many Pets! ♡

Wednesday

Lucy, Hailey, and I were so excited to pet-sit that school flew by! After school, our classmates dropped their pets off at my tree house.

First, we fed them a snack. They all ate really well!

I can't believe you thought this would be difficult, Hailey! They're all being so good!

Then, Diary, it all went a bit wrong . . .

George's snake kept slithering down the toilet.

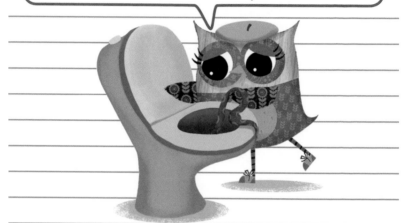

We couldn't get Lilly's moth down from the light bulb.

Zac's spider and Humphrey's spider kept fighting.

Sid and Malcolm, play nice!

Jacob's giant snail left a sticky path all over the couch.

Eww!

Macy's tree frog kept jumping into the fish bowl, which sent Clive, the goldfish, flying.

Zara's crab kept pinching Humphrey.

Oww! Eva, control your pets!

Kiera's bumblebee kept stealing sugar from the kitchen.

And Sue's tortoise kept nibbling on the rug!

But worst of all . . . Baxter STILL didn't play with ANY of them.

By the time everyone had picked up their pets, we were exhausted. And the house was a mess!

Well, one thing's for sure — you're definitely not going to get <u>12</u> pets!

We started cleaning up. I thought about why Baxter didn't want to play with any of the other pets. Normally, he's so playful! I tried to give him a treat to cheer him up. But even that didn't work!

I'm worried about Baxter. Why do you think he's unhappy?

BAT SNAX

Maybe he knows you're getting a new pet! He might be worried you won't love him as much.

Hailey could be right. He is a very smart bat, after all.

You're right! He might not understand my words, but Baxter has always been very good at understanding how I feel.

At bedtime, I finished sewing Baxter's costume for the fashion parade tomorrow. I dressed him up and he smiled. He did a little bow, which made me laugh.

And that's when I realized something . . .
I don't need another pet after all.

I gave him a cuddle. I think he
understood how I felt because he
smiled again and even ate a treat.
As Lucy said, he's a very smart bat.

♡ Pet Fashion Parade ♡

Thursday

Today was the pet fashion parade!

I was a little disappointed about not getting another pet. But the most important thing is to keep my Baxter happy.

At school the pets looked **OWLMAZING**! And Baxter was back to his normal friendly self. He played with everyone!

We flew to the Old Oak Tree. Then the pets paraded past us in their costumes. Don't they all look fabulous, Diary?

But when it was Baxter's turn, he suddenly stopped, sniffed the air, and darted off!

We wondered where Baxter was going. But then we saw him catch up with Lilly's moth. Steve had been trying to chase after a firefly!

Thank you for bringing Steve back! He could have gotten lost.

Everyone clapped.

Well done, Baxter!

He always seems to know when someone needs help!

I was so proud!

Tomorrow is our picnic. I hope Baxter has a great time!

I'm so lucky to have you as my pet!

♡ Picnic Day ♡

Friday

At school we made food for the picnic!

Then we walked to a clearing in the woods. We set up our picnic blankets.

But for some reason, I still wasn't feeling super happy. I love Baxter SO MUCH . . . but I had also <u>really</u> been looking forward to a new pet joining our family.

The picnic was lots of fun! We ate yummy snacks. Then we played games with our pets.

But then, again, Baxter smelled the air and flew off!

BAXTER, WAIT!

We all went looking for him. Finally, we found him playing with a young flying squirrel!

I walked over to them. The little flying squirrel was shy at first. But after I found her an acorn, she liked me. She really likes acorns!

We had so much fun playing together!

Then it was time to go home. I was sad to leave the little flying squirrel.

Bye, cutie! See you again soon!

I started flying away, but Baxter wouldn't come!

Baxter, it's time to go home now. And I'm sure our new friend needs to get back home.

But Baxter started flying up into the tree. I could tell he wanted me to follow him.

He took me to the squirrel's nest. It was empty, except for our new friend.

Oh no.
Does she live here
all alone?

I realized that Baxter already knew the little flying squirrel was on her own. He always seems to know when creatures need help.

In that moment I knew exactly what we should do.

Baxter was so happy, he jumped into the air!

The flying squirrel looked at Baxter and
then back at me. She gave us a big smile!

We flew down to the bottom of the tree.
I told my classmates what had happened.

So it looks like I finally have my new pet!

Everyone cheered. I couldn't wait to bring my new pet home!

When my family met the flying squirrel, they loved her right away. Even Baby Mo!

What <u>am</u> I going to call her, Diary?

I set up a cozy nest next to where Baxter sleeps. I gave my squirrel food and water. And Baxter gave her some of his toys!

She ate her food so quickly!

Wow, you really do love acorns, don't you?

She looked so <u>at home</u> here and Baxter looked really happy.

I reread the list Lucy and I had written for the perfect pet. I ticked every box.

My new pet must be:

☑ Cute

☑ Cuddly

☑ Friendly

☑ Good at playing with Baxter

☑ Not too big (Baxter gets scared easily!)

☑ Not too small (I'd totally lose it!)

I realized that all along, it wasn't that Baxter didn't want me to get a new pet. He wanted to find the <u>right</u> one for both of us. We found a pet that ticked all my boxes, one that he could swoop through the sky with, and one who needed our help.

Oh, I almost forgot to tell you, Diary. I finally chose a name for her!

Sleep well, Acorn. Sleep well, Baxter. Sleep well, Diary.

Rebecca Elliott was a lot like Eva when she was younger: She loved making things and hanging out with her best friends. Now that Rebecca is older, not much has changed — except that her best friends now include her two sons, Benjy and Toby. She still loves making things, like stories, cakes, music, and paintings. But as much as she and Eva have in common, Rebecca cannot fly or turn her head all the way around. No matter how hard she tries.

Rebecca is the author of several picture books, the young adult novel PRETTY FUNNY FOR A GIRL and the bestselling UNICORN DIARIES and OWL DIARIES early chapter book series.

OWL DIARIES

How much do you know about
Eva's New Pet?

Baxter doesn't want to play with
the other pets during show-and-tell
day. Why do you think he is acting
this way? What are two words that
describe how you think Baxter feels?

Look back at the pet fashion
parade on pages 50 and 51. Which
costume is your favorite? Why?

Eva loves how Baxter helps other
animals. What are two ways that
Baxter shows kindness to others
in the story?

Acorn is the perfect pet to join Eva's
family. Why is she the right fit?

Eva has a list of all the things she wants her
new pet to be. What would <u>your</u> ideal pet be?
What personality traits would it have? Draw
and label an image of your dream pet.